Barbie™

Dream, Imagine, Be You

A Book About Everything That Makes You Awesome

Belongs to

Ada Koira

Date

1/7/17

Barbie™

Dream, Imagine, Be You

A Book About Everything That Makes You Awesome

Random House 🏠 New York

WHAT MAKES YOU AWESOME?

My name is _Oda Koiva_

I am _57_ years old.

My birthday is _12/27/58_

My hair color is _Brown_

My eye color is _blue_

I am _5_ feet _4_ inches tall.

4

Draw or paste a picture of yourself here.

Look up, down, backward, and forward to find these words that describe Barbie.

- Creative · Smart · Funny
- Imaginative · Caring · Curious
- Kind · Thoughtful · Brave
- Adventurous

L	U	F	T	H	G	U	O	H	T	A	E
F	G	H	D	B	R	A	V	E	B	C	V
R	C	T	V	C	H	F	X	E	I	R	I
E	U	Q	P	O	S	U	I	O	B	A	T
N	R	S	A	I	D	N	Y	R	A	M	A
G	I	M	A	G	I	N	A	T	I	V	E
N	O	A	K	N	A	Y	M	I	O	H	R
B	U	R	E	R	M	U	D	E	Z	C	C
E	S	T	I	N	D	N	I	K	A	L	F
M	O	Q	S	U	Y	W	Z	A	B	C	M
L	N	P	K	C	A	R	I	N	G	I	J
K	A	D	V	E	N	T	U	R	O	U	S

6

Answer on p. 126

I am...

Barbie lives in Malibu.

Where do you live?_____

How many rooms are in your home?_____

How many steps?_____

How many windows?_____

8

Draw or paste a picture
of your home here.

Where do you want to live when
you grow up? Why?

_____

_____

_____

_____

_____

Barbie loves her room.

The word that best describes my room is

_____.

My room is decorated with _____

_____.

The colors in my room are _____

_____.

If I could change one thing about my
room, it would be _____

_____.

Help decorate Barbie's room.

Draw or paste a picture of your room here.

Barbie's favorite color is pink and
her favorite season is summer.
What are some of your favorites?

My favorite color is_____.

My favorite food is_____.

My favorite TV show is_____.

My favorite movie is_____.

My favorite season is_____.

My favorite sport is _____.

My favorite sports team is _____.

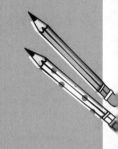

My favorite subject in school is

_____.

My favorite teacher is _____

_____.

My favorite thing to do in school is

_____

_____

_____.

Barbie has many hobbies.

Barbie loves to surf.
Design an awesome surfboard.

Barbie loves to bake.
Help her decorate her cake.

Barbie loves to read.
What are your favorite books?

_____

_____

_____

_____

Write down the things you love to
do in your spare time.

Barbie.

What are three things you are really good at?

1. _____

2. _____

3. _____

Make a list of things you'd like to learn how to do.

_____

_____

_____

_____

_____

_____

The best day ever would be . . .

Barbie

Barbie has three sisters.
Their names are Skipper,
Stacie, and Chelsea.

Who are the people in your family?

I have _____ sisters.

Their names are _____

_____.

I have _____ brothers.

Their names are _____

_____.

How many times can you find the word **FAMILY** in the puzzle below?

```
A  F  A  M  I  L  Y
F  A  M  I  L  Y  F
I  M  L  M  A  F  Y
Y  I  L  I  M  A  F
F  L  A  M  I  M  L
A  Y  F  A  M  I  L
L  F  A  M  I  L  Y
I  L  M  A  F  Y  I
```

27

Answer on p. 126

The thing I love most about
my family is _____

_____

_____

_____

_____

_____

_____

_____

_____

_____.

Draw or paste a picture of your family here.

FAMILY

Skipper loves being a DJ.

Make a playlist of your
favorite songs here.

_____

_____

_____

_____

_____

_____

_____

_____

_____

Stacie loves sports.

Write about your favorite sports memory here.

_____

_____

_____

_____

_____

_____

_____

If you could meet your favorite sports superstar, who would it be?

_____

_____

_____

_____

What questions would you ask him/her?

_____

_____

_____

_____

Chelsea loves to perform.

Use the code below to find out Barbie's advice for her sisters.

H A V E   F U N
A N D   T R Y
Y O U R   B E S T!

A =
H =
E =
V =
U =

F =
N =
D =
T =
S =

R =
Y =
O =
B =

Answer on p. 126

MY FRIENDS

Barbie loves to hang out
with her friends Nikki and Teresa.

Match Barbie and her friends to their shadows.

Answer on p. 126

My Best Friends

Make a list of your best friends here.

_____

_____

_____

_____

_____

_____

List all the things that make your friends special.

_____

_____

_____

_____

_____

_____

_____

_____

Draw or paste a picture
of your friends here.

FRIENDS

Nikki is very artistic.

Write about your most creative
friend here.

Barlie

Nikki is creating a cool dance outfit.

Draw yourself in your favorite dance outfit.

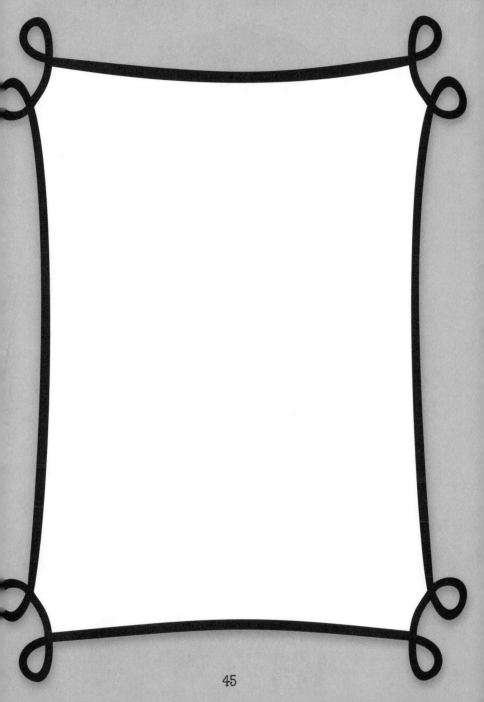

Teresa is Barbie's funniest friend.

Write about your funniest friend here.

_____

_____

_____

_____

_____

_____

_____

_____

_____

_____

_____

Teresa loves
to bake.

Teresa's favorite recipe is her crazy, ooey-gooey chocolate chip cookies. What is your favorite recipe?

Ingredients:

_____

_____

_____

_____

_____

_____

_____

_____

Recipe Directions:

_____

_____

_____

_____

_____

_____

_____

_____

_____

_____

Barbie is helping at the bakery.

Connect the dots to see her sweet treat for you.

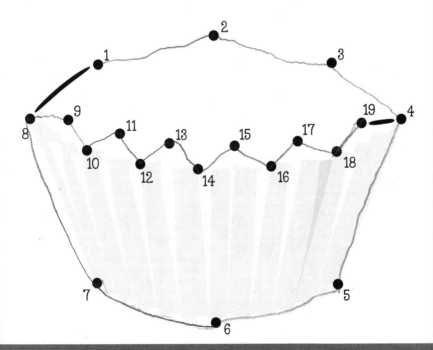

Summer is very sporty.

Write about your most
athletic friend here.

_____

_____

_____

_____

_____

_____

_____

_____

_____

_____

1. SINETN   _____

2. SGUFRNI   _____

3. DVIYSIKGN   _____

4. MSWIGNMI   _____

5. LAVOYELBLL   _____

6. BLAKSELTBA   _____

7. GROCES   _____

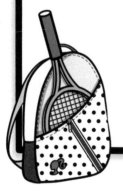

Answer on p. 126

Barbie loves her friends.

What do you love most about your friends?

_____

_____

_____

_____

_____

_____

Barbie and her friends volunteer at the community center. Where would you like to volunteer?

_____

_____

_____

How would you help?

_____

_____

_____

_____

Barbie and her friends always help one another.
Write about a time you helped out a friend.

_____

_____

_____

_____

_____

_____

_____

Write about a time when a friend helped you.

_____

_____

_____

_____

_____

_____

_____

What games do you play
with your friends?

_____

_____

_____

_____

_____

_____

_____

_____

_____

_____

_____

What do you and your friends do when you're together?

_____

_____

_____

_____

_____

_____

_____

_____

_____

_____

Where are your favorite places to hang out with your friends?

_____

_____

_____

_____

_____

_____

_____

_____

_____

A Story You Can Finish with Your Friends!

B

One day, Barbie met up with_____

_____.

They went shopping at _____

_____.

Barbie decided to_____

_____

_____,

and they went to the _____

_____

to get _____

_____.

They went back to Barbie's house.

They made_____

_____

_____.

Suddenly, they heard a strange noise.

It was _____

_____.

Barbie and her friends were so happy

that they decided to _____

_____

_____.

Then they decided to have a sleepover.

They called _____

_____

_____

_____

and they invited _____

_____

_____

_____

_____

_____

_____ .

They danced as they listened to songs
by _____

_____

_____

_____

_____

_____.

They also made their favorite snacks:

_____

_____

_____

_____

_____.

They watched _____

_____

_____

_____

_____

_____.

They stayed up all night playing _____

_____

_____

_____

_____

_____.

dreams

Barbie dreams that she is a fairy.
Draw wings on Barbie.

If a fairy granted you three wishes, what would you wish for?

_____

_____

_____

_____

_____

_____

_____

_____

_____

_____

_____

_____

Barbie flies to imaginary lands.

If you could fly, where would you go?

_____

_____

_____

_____

_____

_____

_____

_____

_____

_____

_____

What would you do as a fairy?

_____

_____

_____

_____

_____

_____

_____

_____

_____

_____

_____

Barbie wishes for a magical pet.
What would your magical pet look like?

How many words can you make using the letters in

FAIRY WINGS?

_____   _____

_____   _____

_____   _____

_____   _____

_____   _____

_____   _____

_____   _____

_____   _____

_____   _____

_____   _____

Answer on p. 126

Teresa dreams of being a mermaid.

Draw a mermaid tail for Teresa.

Draw yourself as a mermaid.

Barbie is a princess.

Draw a tiara for Barbie and
add flowers to her dress.

Barbie has many butterfly friends. Which picture of Barbie is different from the others?

Answer on p. 127

Barbie has many dreams.

What do you dream about?

_____

_____

_____

_____

_____

_____

_____

_____

_____

_____

_____

_____

How many times can
you find the word **DREAM**
in the puzzle below?

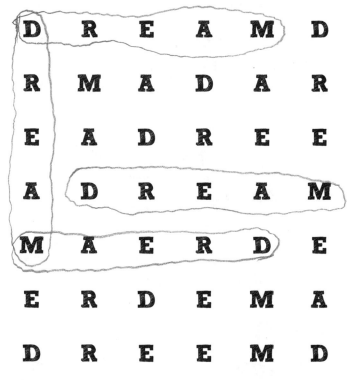

D	R	E	A	M	D
R	M	A	D	A	R
E	A	D	R	E	E
A	D	R	E	A	M
M	A	E	R	D	E
E	R	D	E	M	A
D	R	E	E	M	D

Answer on p. 127

85

iMAGiNE

What YOU could B

Barbie can be anything she wants to be.

CHOICES, CHOICES...

Barbie

· **scientist** · **ballerina**
· **pet vet** · **chef** · **doctor** · **artist**
· **DJ** · **gymnast** · **designer**

```
A   R   C   T   S   A   N   M   Y   G
C   H   E   F   J   L   D   G   F   R
J   D   D   E   S   I   G   N   E   R
E   P   T   Q   X   W   D   E   S   O
S   C   I   E   N   T   I   S   T   T
U   I   R   A   M   L   O   O   S   C
P   E   T   V   E   T   S   T   I   O
A   N   A   S   E   J   R   M   T   D
F   W   V   P   L   Z   A   G   R   N
B   A   L   L   E   R   I   N   A   K
```

Answer on p. 127

Barbie can be a superhero. Her special power is that she can fly.

If you could be a superhero, what would your power or powers be?

_____

_____

_____

_____

_____

_____

_____

_____

_____

_____

_____

_____

_____

Who is your hero? Why?

_____

_____

_____

_____

_____

_____

_____

_____

_____

_____

_____

Write about a time
when you were a hero.

_____

_____

_____

_____

_____

_____

_____

_____

_____

_____

_____

Barbie loves to study marine biology!
What kind of science would you study?

_____

_____

_____

_____

_____

_____

_____

_____

_____

_____

_____

If you were a scientist, what would you invent?

_____

_____

_____

_____

_____

_____

_____

_____

_____

_____

_____

Barbie needs to get to the science lab on time! Find the path to get her there.

START

FINISH

Answer on p. 127

Barbie can be a fashion designer.

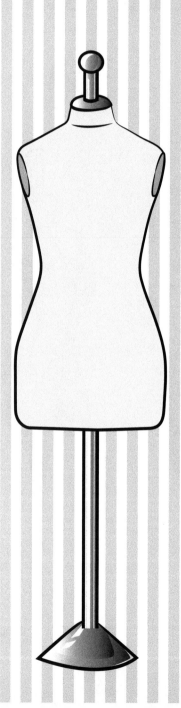

Barbie
can be a
soccer
coach.

Barbie needs to make the goal to win the game. Find the way to the net.

FINISH

START

Answer on p. 12

Barbie can be a pet vet.

Connect the dots to see
Barbie's furry friend.

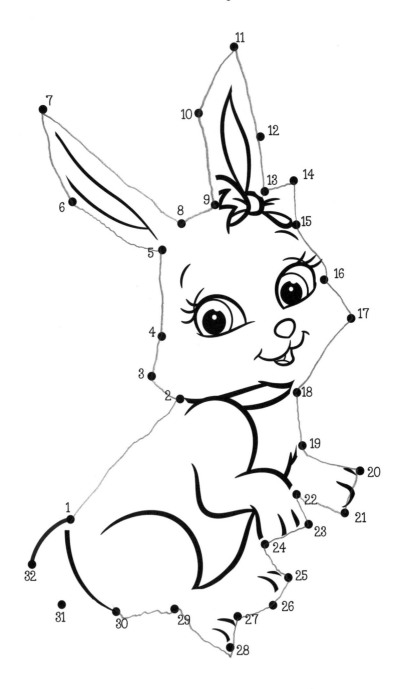

Barbie has lots of pets.

so cute!

Can you match Barbie's pets to their shadows?

Answer on p. 128

What kind of pets do you have?

_____

_____

_____

What are their names?_____

_____

_____

If you could have any animal as a pet, what would you choose? _____

_____

_____

What would you name it? _____

_____

_____

Draw or paste a picture of you and your pet here.

FUR-EVER
FUR-EVER

friends

Barbie and her sisters have adorable puppies!

Connect the dots to see Barbie's pup Taffy.

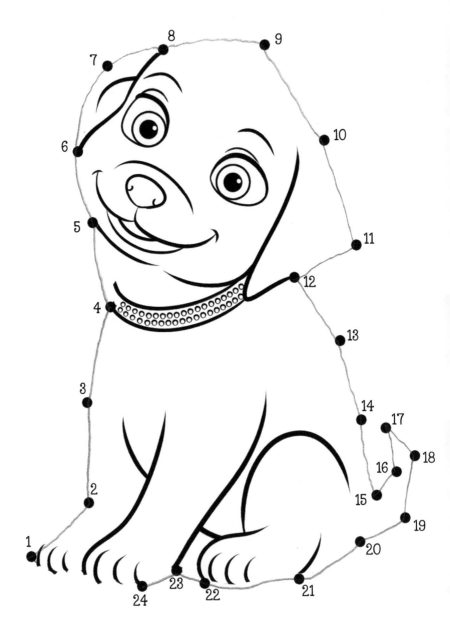

108

Look up, down, backward,
and forward to find the names of
Barbie, her sisters, and their pups.

· **Barbie** · **Skipper** · **Stacie** · **Chelsea**
· **DJ** · **Rookie** · **Taffy** · **Honey**

B	A	R	T	A	F	F	Y
H	S	K	J	A	C	B	D
O	C	S	T	A	C	I	E
N	H	K	F	G	E	H	I
E	E	I	L	P	C	H	R
Y	L	P	I	S	A	D	J
N	S	P	T	X	D	E	Y
W	E	E	I	K	O	O	R
B	A	R	B	I	E	N	I

Answer on p. 128

Barbie can be an artist.

Draw your masterpiece here.

Barbie can be a ballerina.

Draw yourself as a ballerina.

Barbie can be a rock star.

Connect the dots to see what instrument Barbie plays.

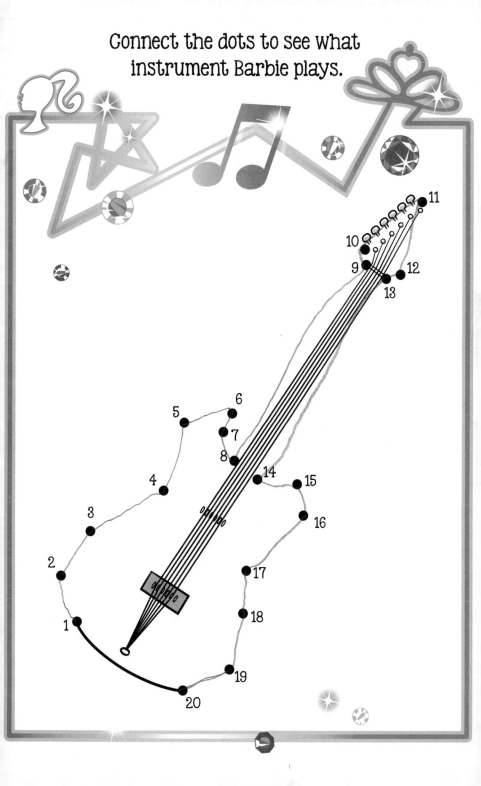

Barbie can be a horse rider.

Draw a pattern on Tawny's
saddle and add bows to her hair.

Barbie can be
a movie star.

Decorate Barbie's new outfit.

Draw yourself as a movie star.

What kind of movies do you like best?

_____

_____

_____

_____

_____

Who are your favorite movie stars?

_____

_____

_____

_____

_____

Use the code below to find out Barbie's message to you.

D R E A M

B I G

B = 

D = 

I = 

R = 

G = 

E = 

M = 

A = 

Answer on p. 128

What do you want to be when you grow up?

_____

_____

_____

_____

_____

One year from now, I will be _____

_____

_____

_____

_____

_____

_____ .

Draw a picture of yourself in the future.

The date I finished this journal is

_V/7/17_

My signature:

Ida Koivu

Barbie GiRL

Answers

Page 6

Page 27

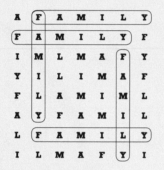

Page 36   Have fun and try your best!

Page 38   A3, B1, C2

Page 54
1. Tennis   5. Volleyball
2. Surfing   6. Basketball
3. Skydiving   7. Soccer
4. Swimming

Page 76   Possible answers: air, airy, fair, fan,
fang, far, fig, fin, gain, gas, nag, nay,
rag, rain, ran, rang, raw, ray, rig, ring,
sag, sang, saw, say, sin, sing, swag,
swan, swig, swing, wag, war, was, way,
wig, win, wing, yarn

Answers

Page 82   B

Page 85

```
D  R  E  A  M  D
R  M  A  D  A  R
E  A  D  R  E  E
A  D  R  E  A  M
M  A  E  R  D  E
E  R  D  E  M  A
D  R  E  E  M  D
```

Page 88

```
A  R  C  T  S  A  N  M  Y  G
C  H  E  F  J  L  D  G  F  R
J  D  D  E  S  I  G  N  E  R
E  P  T  Q  X  W  D  E  S  O
S  C  I  E  N  T  I  S  T  T
U  I  R  A  M  L  O  O  S  C
P  E  T  V  E  T  S  T  I  O
A  N  A  S  E  J  R  M  T  D
F  W  V  P  L  Z  A  G  R  N
B  A  L  L  E  R  I  N  A  K
```

Page 96

127

Answers

Page 100

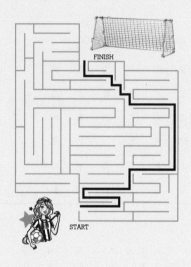

Page 104   A4, B3, C1, D2

Page 109

```
B  A  R  T  A  F  F  Y
H  S  K  J  A  C  B  D
O  C  S  T  A  C  I  E
N  H  K  F  G  E  H  I
E  E  I  L  P  C  H  R
Y  L  P  I  S  A  D  J
N  S  P  T  X  D  E  Y
W  E  E  I  K  O  O  R
B  A  R  B  I  E  N  I
```

Page 122   DREAM BIG